PUFFIN BOOKS

The
Monster Muggs

The Monster Muggs

Jeremy Strong

Illustrated by
Nick Sharratt

PUFFIN BOOKS

Small monsters need big hugs – J.S.

PUFFIN BOOKS

Published by the Penguin Group
Penguin Books Ltd, 80 Strand, London WC2R 0RL, England
Penguin Putnam Inc., 375 Hudson Street, New York, New York 10014, USA
Penguin Books Australia Ltd, Ringwood, Victoria, Australia
Penguin Books Canada Ltd, 10 Alcorn Avenue, Toronto, Ontario, Canada M4V 3B2
Penguin Books India (P) Ltd, 11 Community Centre, Panchsheel Park, New Dehli – 110 0117, India
Penguin Books (NZ) Ltd, Cnr Rosedale and Airborne Roads, Albany, Auckland, New Zealand
Penguin Books (South Africa) (Pty) 24 Sturdee Avenue, Rosebank 2196, South Africa

Penguin Books Ltd, Registered Offices: 80 Strand, London WC2R 0RL, England

www.penguin.com

First published 2000
5 7 9 10 8 6 4

Set in Bembo Schoolbook

Printed in Hong Kong by Midas Printing Ltd

British Library Cataloguing in Publication Data
A CIP catalogue record for this book is available from the British Library

ISBN 0–141–30219–4

The Monster Muggs were very
unhappy. They didn't like their cave.
It was cold and damp. The roof
leaked. Sometimes the wind howled
straight into their front room. The cold
made their feet turn blue. The damp
turned their noses red. The wind gave
them earache. It made their teeth
chatter.

"I don't like it in here," said Little
Mugg. "All we have to keep us warm
is one tiny candle. I'm cold." He
pulled his big ears over his head like a
blanket.

"I'm very cold," shivered Big Mugg.
She wrapped her pigtails round her
neck like a scarf.

"Well, I'm FROZEN STIFF LIKE AN ICICLE!" said Ugly Mugg, shaking his head crossly. "We can't stay in this cave any longer. We must find somewhere warm to live."

"Where can we go?" asked Little Mugg. "Nobody will let us live in a real house."

"We must find somewhere else then,"
said Ugly Mugg. "My bottom is so
cold I think it's going to fall off!"

Ugly Mugg bent over the tiny
candle, but his bottom did not feel any
warmer. He bent lower. All at once his
trousers caught fire.

"Oh! Ho! Eek!" he cried.

Ugly Mugg ran round the cave. Big Mugg and Little Mugg chased after him. They threw water at his trousers. There was a loud *sssss* and the flames went out.

"Oh dear," sighed Ugly Mugg. "Now I have a cold bottom. I've got a hole in my trousers and I'm soaking wet! It's no good. We must find a new house."

So the Monster Muggs set off to find
a new house.

"That old castle looks empty," said
Ugly Mugg.

"That old castle looks creepy," said Little Mugg.

"It's a creepy-heapy!" said Big Mugg. The Monster Muggs crept inside.

Inside the creepy castle it was very dark.

"Come on," said Ugly Mugg. "We are brave monsters. This is a good place to live. I'm not scared. Are you scared, Little Mugg?"

"No," trembled Little Mugg,
covering his eyes with his great big
ears.

"Are you scared, Big Mugg?"

"No," shivered Big Mugg, covering
her eyes with her pigtails.

9

A spider dropped down from the ceiling. It landed on Little Mugg's head.

"Argh! A horrible spider!"

A bat came whizzing round the corner. It landed on Big Mugg's nose.

"Urgh! A horrible bat! I don't like it here!"

A mouse ran up Ugly Mugg's leg.

"Yeeek!" he squeaked. He turned very red and looked at the others.

"I'm not scared," he said. But he was!

AND THEN THREE SPOOKS
CAME INTO THE ROOM!!
  "Whoo!" went Spooky One.
  "Whoo-whooo!" went Spooky Two.
  "Whoo-whooo-whoooooo!!" went
Spooky Three.

"Help!" cried Ugly Mugg. "I'm very scared now! Run for it!"

Little Mugg ran fast and Big Mugg ran faster, but Ugly Mugg was the fastest!

They didn't stop running until they came to a farm. They sat down inside a barn.

"This is better," said Ugly Mugg. "It's nice and quiet in here."

"Honk, honk!"

"Argh! It's a flappy monster with pecky bits," said Big Mugg, and she ran away.

"Moo!"

"Argh! It's a spotty monster with wobbly bits," cried Little Mugg, and he ran away.

Ugly Mugg ran after them. He didn't like being in there on his own.

Ugly Mugg had a bright idea. "I
know somewhere that's warm and dry.
There is plenty of food too. Let's go to
the school!"

"Jelly brain!" cried Big Mugg. "We
can't go there. The school is full of
children."

"No problem! We shall scare them all away," said Ugly Mugg. "We shall pull nasty faces and make horrible noises. The children will be so frightened, they will run away. We shall have the whole school to ourselves. It will be easy."

"Easy-peasy!" laughed Little Mugg.

"Easy-peasy, no more freezy!" shouted Big Mugg.

They set off down the hill.

Down at the school, the playground was full of children. They were running around and laughing and playing. The Monster Muggs hid behind a bush.

"When I say 'GO' we must jump out and frighten them," said Ugly Mugg.

"OK," said Little Mugg.

"Okey-dokey, what a jokey!" said
Big Mugg, laughing.

Ugly Mugg got ready. "GO!" he
yelled.

The Monster Muggs jumped up from behind the hedge. They ran to the playground and they pulled horrible faces.

"BOO!" cried Little Mugg.

"BIG BOO!" bellowed Big Mugg.

"BIG BAD BOO!" shouted Ugly
Mugg, and he made himself go cross-
eyed. He stuck out his tongue. He
pulled out his ears until they hurt.

The children stopped running around the playground and they stared at the Monster Muggs.

"What are you doing?" asked Lucy.

"We're making nasty faces!" growled Ugly Mugg.

"Why are you making nasty faces?" asked Ravi.

"Because we are so scary you are going to run away!" yelled Ugly Mugg.

"You're not scary," said Tracey.

"We're not?" The Monster Muggs were very surprised.

"No, you're not," shouted the children.

"This is scary," said
Ben, and he pulled a
truly horrible face.

"Aaargh!" cried Big
Mugg, jumping back.

"This is scary too," said Anna, and
she stuck out her tongue.

"I want my mummy!" yelled Little
Mugg. He jumped back, right
into Big Mugg's arms.

"And this is even
scarier," said Tom.
He put his fingers in
his mouth and pulled
his lips wide.

24

"Let's get out of here!" screamed
Ugly Mugg. He jumped right back
into Little Mugg's arms.

Big Mugg ran and ran. She was still
carrying the other two Muggs, and the
children chased after them. Big Mugg
ran round to the back of the school.

"Quick, hide in here!" cried Ugly
Mugg. They jumped inside a giant
rubbish bin and hid beneath the
rubbish.

"Phew!" sighed Big Mugg. "We're
safe now."

Ugly Mugg looked round the inside
of the bin. It was dark and warm
inside. There was no wind freezing his
bottom off. There was no rain dripping
through the roof. He looked at Big
Mugg and Little Mugg and gave them
a big smile.

"Welcome to our new home!" he
said.

Also available in First Young Puffin

DUMPLING
Dick King-Smith

Dumpling wishes she could be long and sausage-shaped like other dachshunds. When a witch's cat grants her wish Dumpling becomes the longest dog ever.

ERIC'S ELEPHANT ON HOLIDAY
John Gatehouse

When Eric and his family go on holiday to the seaside, Eric's elephant goes too. Everyone is surprised – and rather cross – to find a big white elephant on the beach. But the elephant soon amazes them with her jumbo tricks and makes it a very special holiday indeed!

GOODNIGHT, MONSTER
Carolyn Dinan

One night Dan can't get to sleep. First of all he sees a strange shadow on the wall. Then he sees huge teeth glinting and hairy feet under the bed. It couldn't really be a monster – could it?